Naeem Murr

NUDE

D1403678

Naeem Murr's first novel, *The Boy*, was a *New York Times* Notable Book. Another novel, *The Genius of the Sea*, was published in 2003. His latest, *The Perfect Man*, was awarded The Commonwealth Writers' Prize for the Best Book of Europe and South Asia, and was long-listed for the Man Booker Prize. His work has been translated into eight languages. He has received many awards for his writing, most recently a Guggenheim Fellowship and a PEN Beyond Margins Award. Born in London, he now makes his home in Chicago.

First published by GemmaMedia in 2012.

GemmaMedia
230 Commercial Street
Boston, MA 02109 USA

www.gemmamedia.com

© 2012 by Naeem Murr

Printed in the United States of America

16   15   14   13   12   1   2   3   4   5

978-1-936846-07-8

Library of Congress Cataloging-in-Publication Data

Murr, Naeem.
    Nude / Naeem Murr.
       p. cm. — (Gemma open door)
    ISBN 978-1-936846-07-8
    I. Title.
    PR6063.U73624N83 2012
    823'.914—dc23
                        2011053246

Cover by Night & Day Design

Inspired by the Irish series of books designed for adult literacy, Gemma Open Door Foundation provides fresh stories, new ideas, and essential resources for young people and adults as they embrace the power of reading and the written word.

Brian Bouldrey
North American Series Editor

GEMMA
Open Door

For
Peter Stitt
and
The Gettysburg Review
with deep gratitude

ONE

The cashier in Tesco clutched Eugene's arm, fearing he might collapse again. She must have seen him many times, a willowy old man in his mackintosh and trilby hat. While scanning his Toblerone, sardines, and Ovaltine, she might have been struck by the Wedgwood blue of his eyes; eyes that somehow took her in without being so bold as to look at her.

Eugene, trying to steady himself, was just glad she'd not seen him steal the poster from the notice board. On it was an etching he'd recognized, a nude, but not for the life of him had he been able to remember who the artist was. He'd been furious, having lectured on this very etching as an art teacher at the Sacred Heart. As he'd slipped it into his pocket for later, the artist's name had tugged tantalizingly at one of the many lines he'd cast out into the fog. That's when he'd felt it—like a sudden blow—and fainted.

"Two left feet," he insisted, snatching up his shopping bag and hurrying out. What's wrong with me? He walked quickly. Last week, in line at the post office, he'd felt a sensation like two hands unfurling gently as smoke to take hold of the back of his head. Next thing he knew, he'd landed on a screaming toddler. Bad circulation. Maybe he should have stayed on at the Galerie des Beaux Arts, but it would have killed him to sell another insipid Thames-view watercolor to one of Richmond's *nouveau riche*. Not working made him anxious, though, which probably explained this low-level headache he couldn't seem to shake.

Soon he was at his tower block on the Roehampton Council Estate. He hated using the lift, which stank of urine and was littered with condoms and bags of glue, but he was on the seventeenth floor. It came to him the second he shut his front door. *Rembrandt.* He snatched the poster from his pocket. Of course! That lusty face, the imprint of a garter around her meaty thigh. To see it better, he took a seat at his kitchen table, which was in front of a window. Along the sill stood a half-dozen of the brightly colored antique bottles his wife used to collect, a tiny embryo of light in each. Below the picture it said, Open Figure Drawing, £5, no instructor, Wednesday at eight, Wharf Thirteen.

Once, imitating the ghostly naturalism of Ferrazzi's *Idol of the Prism*, he'd painted his wife, nude, right at this table.

She was holding one of these bottles—red—in front of her face. He'd sketched her face around and through it, and, as her arm had grown tired, had followed its lurid tracer down over her right breast and belly to where she brought it to rest between her legs. Catherine. He still longed for her, and thought now of the beauty marks on her back, her tiny, slightly spoon-shaped toes. That had been his last painting.

He'd not done many nudes. It struck him now how few naked bodies he'd ever seen. Amanda Collinger was the first, a blind spinster in her mid-thirties. As a boy, she gave him two bob every Saturday to polish her silver, letting him listen to the radio, her fat old guide dog, Dillinger, curled at his feet. (It wouldn't be long before he would help her bury Dillinger beneath her horse chestnut.) One time he realized he'd forgotten to bring down the carriage clock in her bedroom. He sprinted up the stairs, past the bathroom where she was having a bath, and into her room. As he took hold of the clock, Amanda entered in her robe, removing it before he could say anything, and closing the door. Taking a seat at her dresser, she rubbed lotion into her skin. Her body was perfectly pear-shaped, with small upturned breasts that put him in mind of thorns.

A body not at all like those in the dirty magazines his older brother, Simon, hid behind their wardrobe. Women with their eyes closed, mouths open, suckling on fantasies of men more impressive than those who looked at them. Men like his dad, who brought women home from the pubs when his mum was on night shift at the Samaritans. One night Eugene had been shaken awake into the sight of his dad's hairy beer belly hanging over his Y-fronts. Eugene followed him into his parents' bedroom. Sprawled naked on her back on the bed lay his school friend Derek's widowed mum, vomit all over the pillow. "Is she dead, tell me?" His dad was terrified. "Take a listen to her ticker. Can't hear a bloody thing with my tinnitus." Pale scars, like cirrocumulus, fanned out over her belly; her breasts had pooled flat into the pits of her arms. Eugene put his ear gently to her chest, which smelled of his dad's hands, a fishmonger's hands, scrubbed with halves of lemon. Nothing for a moment, and then, like the distant scuff of oars, her heart.

His mum was next. It upset him to bring this back to mind. His little sister died because the hand pump they used to drain her water-on-the-brain had malfunctioned. A week later, his mum, drunk, fell down the stairs, dislodging a disk. She begged his dad to get her sister in. "What for?" he said, adding as he jerked his head toward Eugene, "This little girl will look after you." For weeks she lay on the living room floor, sometimes drugged so senseless with painkillers that she messed herself. Eugene cleaned her, brought her bedpans, and hooked up the machine that emptied her breasts, with those beautiful blue veins, of their milk. She would scream at him to keep his eyes shut. When he had no choice but to see what he was doing, she would close her own eyes.

After this, only three more: Queenie, Catherine, and Lisa—his Galatea—that poor girl.

Time for his shower. He got up from the table, but a little too quickly, and felt as if he'd hit a low ceiling. As he walked toward the bathroom, slipping off his coat, his head was like a boat's hold in which cargo had come unsecured. The old pipes clamored as he turned the squeaky tap for the shower. He pulled down the toilet lid and sat, waiting for the water to heat up. Wretched. A wretched day—though it would have been a good deal more so if Queenie had seen him collapse. She had tapped his shoulder just as he'd put his shopping down to examine the notice board this morning.

"What you looking for, love?" she said.

"Youth."

"Me?" She smiled.

"Youth," he repeated, louder.

Propping her reading glasses on her nose, she surveyed the board while he surveyed her. Though she was black Irish, most had taken her for Italian in her youth, a mass of dark curls (now iron gray) around a face of coarse features that had no business being so lovely. Her eyes, the green of weathered copper, seemed never to blink. She had lived two doors down; they were close friends as children, entering their teenage years during the war. One night an air raid shattered all the windows in his house as he and his family huddled beneath the kitchen table. The next morning Queenie fetched him out. She led him around roadblocks and up to the third floor of a half-collapsed building, motioning for him to look out the window. On a pile of rubble lay a sapper beside an unexploded bomb, touching it so tenderly it might have been a lover. "Bloody hell!" Eugene flung himself into the room and tried to get out, but she jerked him back. "Why are you always so scared?" She released him, but he stayed. As the sapper breathlessly drew the fuse from that naked bomb, he glanced at Queenie: she looked as if she had found (and it horrified her) her vocation; found and lost it at once.

They fell back into the room. He began to cry, at which she couldn't stop herself laughing. She kissed him (out of pity, she would admit years later), keeping her eyes open so he had to close his. In that room he discovered himself in her body, slender and so sensitive. It was as if the souls of each were the bodies of the other, she a boy struggling to reclaim her own nakedness from him, he a girl struggling to reclaim his from her.

She was engaged to William even then. A childish promise, she told Eugene, given in the heat of his leaving, the nearest she could get, until her brother joined up a year later, to having some part of herself at the front. On the same day that William's mother told her he'd been sent to a mental hospital in Belgium, her family received a telegram informing them that her brother had been killed at Anzio. She buzz-cut her hair, put on her brother's overalls, and tried to enlist, causing a frightful scene. William returned a shell-shocked wreck; under pressure of her guilt and that English decency that seemed to be what everyone had suffered and died for, she married him.

The groom was trembling too much in the church to put the ring on her finger, though not half as much as Eugene, who sat in a pew at the back quietly tearing pages out of the hymn book.

She'd wanted to sacrifice herself to the war. Now, in an empty and unconsummated marriage, she had. Eugene had hated her at first, but she had what was his, and he what was hers. Everyone knew. Eugene, who didn't have a place of his own, often went to Queenie's house, and they would make love downstairs as William lay upstairs, embalmed in Mahler like an insect in amber. In those years she had his nakedness still, and he hers, but it had become a sadder, more labored nakedness, like a beautiful clockwork machine that created the illusion of nakedness in its motion, but was now, slowly, running down.

In the supermarket, Queenie took off her glasses and turned back to him. "You should try the notice board at Harrods," she said. "Tesco's a bit down-market for something like Youth."

He smiled. How little, really, she'd changed.

"There's ballroom dancing at the Center tomorrow, Euge."

"I'll join the danse macabre only when I have no choice, Queenie."

Smiling wanly, she took his hand. "I heard you fainted in the post office."

"Men don't faint, we're felled like great trees in—"

"For God's sake." She tightened her hold, those green eyes anxious and questioning. She was going to say something else but contained herself.

"Come to the Center tomorrow," she said finally. Discarding his hand along with that useless fragment of language, she left.

Steam clouded the mirror above his sink. He felt shaky, at the edge of tears again, fearful, that rogue cargo of memory loose in his hold. He looked up to see the water sputtering from the showerhead and remembered why he was here. He stood and stepped into the shower, tugging back the plastic curtain. Still consumed by his thoughts of Queenie, it took a few moments for him to feel uncomfortable. What have I forgotten? He looked down to see the cuffs of his trousers, soaked and clinging to his sopping shoes.

TWO

Eugene hurried through the park, worried they might close Richmond Gate. The air was thick with the brackish odor of the ferns. The trees sponged in what little light remained, turning the few people he came upon into Seurat's grainy shades. Pushing down his trilby and pulling up the collar of his mackintosh against the chill, he tried not to think about the skin of soaking clothes he'd left on the bathroom floor.

The restlessness in the breeze of the trees beside the path made Eugene think of something his wife had once told him about how it felt, when she was on night duty during the war, to walk through hospital wards of wounded soldiers sleeping.

Where was Catherine tonight? Had she forgiven him for what had happened all those years ago with Lisa, his student? Lisa, whose pale skin would flush so she looked scalded if he so much as glanced at her in class. He caught sight of Lisa in the street sometimes, walking as if through an endless gauntlet of jeering men. He wanted to tell her there was power in her body, but it wasn't his place.

That he should have lost his job, his wife. His life.

Once through the gate, he made his way down to the Thames and sat on a bench near Richmond Bridge. Jimmy would pass here on his way to the Duke. He just wanted someone to talk to, though he knew Jimmy would shy from talk that even flirted with intimacy. But Jimmy was one of the most sensitive and thoughtful men

Eugene had ever known. If there were anyone in Eugene's acquaintance who might
have achieved greatness, it was Jimmy. His
acclaimed doctoral thesis on the human
body of Christ had been followed, during
his first year of seminary in Dublin, by a
book of poems that many had compared
to the work of Hopkins. How had he al-
lowed himself to become just an old man
obsessed with his bowels? Ever since he'd
left the Jesuits and come to England, just
after the war, he'd led a dissolute life. He
spent most nights in the Duke, and when
he was younger worked his way, as if he
didn't much care for the job but needed
the overtime, through one woman after
another. Women drawn, no doubt, to his
gentle and unavailable soul.

It was dark before Eugene saw him
coming down the towpath, that massive,

shambling frame. He looked like an old bare-knuckle fighter, now ruined and brooding.

"Euge," Jimmy called out, his voice still carrying a faint Dublin lilt, "you're looking very metaphysical tonight."

"Am I?"

"You are, indeed." Jimmy cut over and sat himself beside Eugene. "You should try to get a grant from the city council for sitting here and looking profound. They could make you a tourist attraction. Sure, the Americans will pay for anything."

"Why not?" Eugene was overwhelmed, as always, by Jimmy's jokey chatter.

"Hey, you should come to the Duke tonight," Jimmy continued. "Gary's in town. All the old gang will be there."

"Yes, I might."

"God, it's been years since I've seen

you in the Duke. You're becoming a bit of a recluse."

Jimmy lit a cigarette. It was Eugene's opportunity to speak, but he didn't want to banter. He wanted to tell Jimmy he'd just got into the shower with all his clothes on. He didn't care if Jimmy made a joke of it; Jimmy would understand he was afraid. But he couldn't just say it straight out like that, and Jimmy's discomfort at the silence, his fidgeting and checking of his watch compounded Eugene's reluctance, until, to relieve the tension, Eugene blurted, "So how's your stomach?"

"My bowels, you mean?" Shaking his head, he declared with genuine feeling, "Euge, if you could know how much I envy those who have a smooth and regular motion. I can go weeks without going, *weeks*. People don't even say, 'How've you been, Jimmy?' anymore; they say, '*Have* you been, Jimmy?' It's getting embarrassing. Do you think I'm obsessed?"

"Dedicated's the word I'd use, Jim," Eugene said.

Jimmy took a drag and sighed out the smoke. "Well, I take solace from the fact that most great men have trouble with their bowels. Savonarola blamed it on continuous intellectual labor. Aquinas, Monet, Sartre—bowels like a miser's fist, the lot of them. Martin Luther had two enemas a day and Gauguin had to be treated all his life for chronic piles."

They fell into silence for a moment. Eugene's desperation to speak and his sensitivity to Jimmy's almost pathological fear of anything but the comic or banal caused his heart now to beat up into his throat.

"Do you know what I did today?" he finally got out.

Jimmy cracked the fingers of his massive hands.

"I got into the shower—"

Frowning, Jimmy stared into the dark water of the Thames, now covered in small slicks of light from the streetlamps on the far bank. Eugene realized he probably knew about the incident in the post office. The pulse in his throat entered his head, his skull beginning to throb like a bad tooth.

"Now your brother," Jimmy said at last, "I've no doubt had the most satisfactory relationship with water closets— not that he wasn't a great man, you understand. He was. A leader of men. But artless, natural. Fearless. Only boy, so I heard, wasn't afraid of Gary."

"Gary always got the worst of it when they fought," Eugene agreed.

"You see—now *there's* a man who never betrayed his body. Met him a few times. Funny as the devil, he was—well, I don't need to tell you that. Colon supple as a snake, I bet."

They fell silent again.

"You're right," Eugene took up finally, the pain in his head now acute. "He was a man of the body. That's why he did what he did."

Jimmy nodded, saying quickly under his breath, "Well, it was a tragedy, sure. Those people should have been made to pay for doing that to him."

"It was a joke." Eugene hoped he might feel some reproach in these words.

Jimmy nodded gently, stamped out

his cigarette, and stood. "Come to the pub," he said.

"I might a little later. I just want to sit here for a while." Sickness welled in his stomach.

Jimmy stared down at him, his gentle, brutal face sorrowful, almost wincing. For a moment he seemed to be on the verge of speaking, but finally just nodded and walked away.

THREE

Eugene stood outside the Duke. After Jimmy had left, he'd lain down on the bench until the sickness and headache had subsided. He was nervous. Right after what happened with Lisa it had been impossible to go into a local. In The Spur once, when Eugene ordered a half, the barman walked into the gents with a glass, returning to set it, full of urine, in front of him. The pub exploded in applause. But he didn't want to return yet to his dark flat and that pile of wet clothes.

Gary, Terry, Jimmy and William stood at the far end of the bar, Jimmy animatedly telling a story in which the refrain was a raucous "Don't cry for me Argentina!" Apart from the barman—a young Sikh— the pub was empty. The boy's sullen approach toward Eugene drew the attention of the other men.

" 'ear, 'ear," Gary's deep, rasping voice boomed through the pub, "it's Van Goff." Gary was a squat barrel of a man, opulently bald, wearing a Burberry coat and smoking a Monte Cristo.

"No, no, no," Terry countered with

peevish relish. "It's that Italian chappie, the one who did the *Moan*-a Lisa."

"Shut it," Gary said fiercely, causing Terry to sink his head into his collar like a chided schoolboy. Terry was a scrawny, rodent-faced man of sixty who used boot polish to dye his little mustache and had worn the same threadbare tweed sporting jacket for the past twenty years.

Queenie's husband, William, that wintry wreck of a man, looked over at Eugene with a grieved, apologetic expression, his blue eyes lifeless as glass. Jimmy frowned down into his drink, trying to deny anything painful, as always.

Hurt more by this pity than by Terry's cruelty, Eugene curtly ordered a J&B and didn't move any closer to the men.

But Gary rapped his heavy gold rings against the bar. "Put his drink over here,

Sunshine," he called to the barman, and threw down a couple of pounds.

"I really am in the most awful rush," Eugene called.

"Oh how *ouful* are those *ouful* rushes that one so *oufton* finds oneself in, don't you know," Gary said, grinning incorrigibly for a moment before his upper dentures slipped in his mouth. Eugene had never understood why Gary, with all his money, wore that ill-fitting set of National Health dentures, which he never properly adhered to his gums.

As Eugene, resigned, went over to join them, Jimmy slapped his hand joyfully on the bar and called out to the young Sikh, "The prodigal returns. Bring me a fatted calf."

"Fatted calf?" the Sikh said. "Only mixed drink I know's a snakebite."

"Stop insulting him," William hissed at Jimmy. "Hardly kosher is it, fatted calves."

"He's not Jewish, you senile old twat," Terry said.

"What'd you call him?" Gary said indignantly. "This man was on the Normandy beaches while you were sucking on your mum's teat."

Terry, cowed again, drew his mustache into his mouth, staining his lips.

Gary then turned to Eugene and said with a look of paternal concern, "Now, my old muck, what you been up to, ay?"

"Playing the stock market, yachting in the Caribbean, advising on covert military operations, the usual things, Gary," Eugene answered, suavely, he thought.

Smiling, Gary chewed the end of his cigar. "You flogged any masterpieces lately?"

"Not my line anymore, selling amateur rubbish to rich fools."

"Must be hard for a genius such as yourself," Terry cut in snidely under his breath.

"Exactly," Jimmy snatched up in a bright, comic tone. And, turning so he was facing away from the other men, he responded as if someone were interviewing him: "Eugene Butler? Well, of course I've known him since he was a skittering little whelp. But you could always tell he was a genius because he smelled bad and never knew what day it was. You see, he—"

"Ay, Sunshine?" Gary called to the Sikh, cutting Jimmy off. "When's Rita getting 'ere?" He didn't like anyone else to take center stage for too long.

The Sikh, now reading *The Mirror*, shrugged.

"The new girl," Gary explained. "You should see her, Euge." Cupping his fat hands out in front of him, he smacked his lips.

"That girl can find out what I have on tap any time," Terry added in an emphatic whisper, an errant tear running down to his mustache, then drawing a dark line from there to his chin.

Jimmy joined the chorus of praise. "I've said it a hundred times: her eyes are the *exact* gray of the sky over County Clare. I just have to look at her and I can feel the rain—"

"Which in Ireland," Gary mocked in a massacred brogue, "is the warm tears of the suffering saints themselves!"

A glass shattered on the floor.

Gary called to the Sikh, "Sunshine, get 'im another one, ay."

The Sikh swept up the glass.

"It was greasy, I think," Eugene said, rubbing his fingers together and avoiding the glances being passed around the men. He felt so fragile suddenly. For a moment he'd forgotten he had the glass in his hand.

William spoke. "You been all right, Euge?" he said in his brittle old voice. "Queenie said you'd collapsed."

His pitying tone infuriated Eugene. "What is this, the event of the year in Roehampton? I trip over in the post office and everyone thinks I'm a closet alcoholic."

"I didn't mean anything by it." William mustered what he could of indignation in his trembling face.

These men all believed they knew his life, knew him. They knew nothing.

Nothing but this empty and obscene banter ever passed between them.

"Rita, Rita, Rita." Once more Jimmy tried to smooth things over, his rhapsodic voice embarking softly into the painful silence. "Now there's a subject for a great work of art. How would you paint her, Eugene? Eyes like the rain, hair like . . . something, her body like . . . something else. She's poetry!"

"She's a tasty little tart, is what she is," Gary said, chewing greedily on his dentures.

"For God's sake," Eugene said, sickened, "she'd as soon look at your sagging old backsides as at your faces."

"You're full of poison tonight, aren't you," Gary said, coloring now.

"Well, why do you all have to stand in

here baying at the moon? Look at your-
selves. *You're old men.*"

"And I'm bloody proud of it, mate,"
Gary barked back. "I come from nothing.
Now I got a boat in Yarmouth, villa in
Majorca, Jag. Bill 'ere was on the beaches
at Normandy, blown to kingdom come
and back he was. Jimmy wrote books,
speaks La'in, Greek. Terry . . ." Now he
had to tread water furiously, trying to
think of something to recommend Terry.
"He's a good mate if he don't drink. And
what have *you* ever done, ay?"

"What have *I* ever done?" Eugene
faltered, fell silent. The atmosphere was
excruciating.

"Talking about tasty tarts," Terry
slurred, aware only that no one was speak-

ing, "anyone see the poster in Tesco? Nude model, Wharf Thirteen—privates open to the public, no less."

"Probably some old slapper," Gary said viciously, venting what remained of his anger.

Terry raised his brows and pursed his lips as if to consider this. "Well, the woman on the poster wasn't exactly Twiggy, but—"

"It was a Rembrandt," Eugene said with forced calm, trying desperately to think of a way to explain to Gary, to all of them, exactly what he'd ever done.

"You saw it too?" Gary said.

"I was interested in the etching."

"I bet you were."

"Now don't cast aspersions, Gary,"

Jimmy playfully warned, though his glance moved cautiously between the two men. "Eugene's an aesthete."

"An es-what?"

"One who lives by the eye," Jimmy explained.

"He's a dirty old esfeet is what he is," Gary said, smiling now, appeased.

"I taught that etching," Eugene began—here it was, he felt: Rembrandt's nude, a loose thread from his past, might unravel his life. "If you look closely—"

"I went out with a model once," Terry interrupted. "Beautiful, she was. Beeutiful."

"Went out with a model? Hark at him, the Don Juan of East Wapping," Gary said.

"No, no, he's right," Jimmy took up with apparent defensiveness. "I remember her well. She modeled nylon dressing gowns in the windows at Woolworth's. Sure, she was *gorgeous*—and when you took her arms off, she did the greatest impression of the Venus de Milo."

While they got back into the rhythm of their banter, Eugene's eyes settled on William, who was emitting the oddest squeals of delight. There he was, the man whom he'd once wished dead every day of his life. He glanced around at the other men. They all knew of his affair with Queenie, believed they knew about Lisa too, pitied him for it, and were perhaps a little repulsed also. The shame burned in Eugene as he stared at their laughing faces, holding the drink that Gary had bought for him. It was all so false.

"So, William," Terry cut into the raucous laughter, trying to shift the focus of

Gary and Jimmy's playful scorn off himself, "where's Queenie tonight?"

"What d'you want to know for?" Gary said, instantly protective of William.

"Well, she don't as a rule let him out late of an evening, does she. You been a naughty boy, Willy?" Terry spoke as if to an infant. "Have you been a bad boy?"

"Queenie was so beautiful, wasn't she?" Eugene addressed himself directly to William, who was glowering at Terry, his look as close to fierce as his fragile old features could muster. Eugene couldn't stand it anymore, these lies.

"Very small," was all William would concede, with a suspicious glance.

"Women should be small," Gary declared, obviously worried about Eugene's intentions.

"Do you remember when she tried to enlist?" Eugene said.

"I was in the wars," William said, using the phrase mothers use when their children come to them with a scraped knee: *You been in the wars, love?* Perhaps this was the only way he could get the word out, Eugene thought. At last, he'd touched something real in this place.

"Course they knew straight away she wasn't a man." Though Eugene felt a deep qualm, he had to go on. "But you know I've often imagined her getting through somehow, right to the end, where the recruits stand naked in front of the draft board. I mean, can't you just see it? Young man after young man, and then . . . Queenie." Eugene stared hard into William's hazy, timid old face, those glassy blue eyes.

"We didn't have to take off our underwear," William said with an angry and stubborn frown.

"I think you're letting your imagination get away with you, Eugene," Gary said, his tone like a dog's guttural growl.

But Eugene couldn't stop himself. "I was in love with Queenie, you know, William. Queenie and I were in love. For years we—"

"I know that," William almost shouted, his gaunt face coloring, his eyes widening with disbelief and fear. "I know that."

The bar door swung open and a squat blonde woman walked in.

"Sorry I'm late, love," she called to the Sikh, who, sullen as ever, folded his paper and ambled out.

All the men's eyes were instantly fixed on this woman, whose appearance had saved them. She wore a cream blouse, a red leather skirt, and black tights. Eugene noticed a run in the tights, behind her knee, the faint gloss of nail varnish dabbed at its two extremities. Brushing out her bleached hair, she scrutinized herself in the mirror behind the shelf of spirits. After applying lipstick, she tried to pull away but lingered, as if reluctant to lose sight of someone she loved and might never see again. Finally, she turned to the men with opened arms.

"What do you think?" she said.

"Don't cry for me Ar-gen-tin-a," Jimmy belted out, causing Terry and Gary to laugh—Terry uproariously, Gary somewhat more subdued, obviously still troubled by Eugene's outburst.

After cutting her eyes at them, she glanced at Eugene. "Who's this then?"

"Eugene Butler," Gary said coldly. "He's an esfeet."

"Is that another word for an actor?" she said.

"I worked in a gallery," Eugene cut in quickly, "selling paintings."

"Oh, that must have been nice for you," she said with motherly indulgence.

She rested her hands on the bar, their blood-red nails splaying like little fans from her stubby fingers. Eugene looked into her face, which was very much like that of the woman in the Rembrandt: plump, kindly, rather obtuse. She'd plastered a thick, grainy base over her bad skin, and he saw now that her youth lay all but dead. Obviously troubled by his scrutiny, she looked back at the other men.

Snatching up her hand, Gary placed it, as it formed a fist, to his lips.

"Get off with ya," she said playfully, pulling free just as the bar door swung open again. This time it revealed Queenie. Terry smiled.

"How foolish of me," Queenie said dryly, fixing a hard gaze on William. "And how thoughtless. When you told me, four hours ago, that you were going out to get a loaf—" Just then she saw Eugene, which caused her to falter and blush. Quickly she mustered herself. "When you told me you were going out to get a loaf, it didn't occur to me that someone as deeply pious as yourself, my dearest, must have the blood as well as the body of Christ."

"What you drinking, darlin'?" Gary asked, nervously rubbing his hands together.

"Gin tonic, my love," she said.

"Well, Eugene," she went on with

feigned indifference, plucking off her gloves. "Haven't seen you here for a while."

"He's been a hair trigger all bloody night, love," Gary said.

Rita put Queenie's gin and tonic on the bar. "If you need anything else, I'll be in the cellar. Give me a shout," she said. Pulling up the cellar door, she disappeared.

Terry pointed his pinkie at Eugene: "He's been fantasizing about you naked, Queenie."

"Sounds more like a nightmare," Queenie said.

"No disrespect," Gary shivered his back as he stared hungrily into the open cellar hatch, "but there's nothing in this world like a firm young body."

"Well, Eugene would know about that," Terry said.

"Shut up," Gary shouted. "That's all over now."

"It's not over," Eugene said, infuriated far more by Gary's delicacy than Terry's cruelty. "But what's sad is you're all worse than I am. What's sad is I'm suffering for you."

Gary stared at him, too amazed for a moment even to be angry.

Again Eugene couldn't stop himself. "None of you ever say anything in here, do you? You never actually *say* anything. Why d'you even bother? Why don't you just bark like a pack of dogs? I've known you all my life, Gary"—now he turned specifically to Gary—"but what do I know really? I know your son keeps some interesting company. I know you loved your wife, Dove, that we all talk about her as if she's dead when really she's living with—"

"Don't you fucking dare," Gary shouted, spittle sparking from his mouth, his dentures slipping.

"For the love of God, just let's calm down," Jimmy said, though he knew it was too late and had already pushed his body between the two men as Gary, his face white with fury, hurled himself forward. Gary's swinging hand hit Eugene's face, but at the same time he struck his own throat against Jimmy's shoulder and the impact made him spit out his dentures. Quickly, Queenie retrieved them from the floor and stood protectively in front of Eugene, holding the teeth up toward Gary in her open hand like a peace offering. Though he still feigned to be straining to get at Eugene, sputtering curses, the fight had gone out of Gary; his face, now red, was closer to tears than to fury and grotesquely aged by the loss of his teeth.

Eugene was steadying himself against the bar, pressing his hand to his cheek, though it had been a glancing blow. Terry stood, staring into his glass, as if he were completely alone in the pub, and William was shaking almost uncontrollably. Finally, Queenie got Gary to take back his teeth and turned to Eugene as if he were an upset child who was neither hers nor particularly appealing.

His teeth now back in, Gary shouted over Jimmy's shoulder. "What were you, eh? You were a school teacher bloody touched up your pupils, that's what you were."

Eugene stared into Queenie's eyes. For the first time in all the years he had known her, she looked away. He whispered, "I'm dying, Queenie."

Her expression became stony. "You've done enough now," she said. "Go home."

FOUR

The next morning, Eugene woke very late. There was a tingling sensation all down his left arm and a dry ache in his head. This was part of a still-clinging dream, his throbbing heart recalling to him the opening and closing of gills. The dream was a childhood memory of coming upon a red-haired boy fishing at Pen

Ponds. Half a dozen fish lay on the grass beside him in the sun. "Why don't you kill them?" Eugene asked, squatting over the fish. "They'll die," the boy said simply, as if Eugene were being impatient. There was something strange about the way the boy spoke, as if he had a lisp. Eugene looked up into his freckled, squinting face, and the boy very slowly pushed out his tongue. On it lay a live maggot. "Keeps 'em warm," the boy said. "The fish like that." It took Eugene a while to get out of bed, for his heart to struggle back to its shallow, fouled pool. The tingling in his arm persisted. I must have slept on it. He really felt out of sorts. Perhaps he was coming down with the flu and should stay home, but tonight was the open figure drawing.

Anticipation of this gave form to his

time. Slowly his flat would fill up with his sketches. I might even start painting again, he thought, sell them up at Hyde Park. Who knows, perhaps I could find a niche even among the great, as Lowry did, late in life. An image flashed into his mind of that red-haired boy, his tongue extended, upon it a tiny nude as exquisite as the one by Fortuny he'd seen in Barcelona. Too grotesque, he realized; still, he was thrilled at the thought of what might come from a mind released of its own constraints.

According to the radio, thunderstorms were on the way, but the morning seemed painted by Janet Fish, all liquid sunlight. Impatient for the evening, Eugene went all the way into town to buy a sketchbook and pencils, then treated himself to tea and cake at a Knightsbridge café. After returning home for a light dinner, he left his flat at five for Wharf Thirteen, which would take him a good couple of hours along the towpath.

The riverside at Richmond was packed with people making the best of this bright day, but, slow as a cataract, dark clouds closed in from the east. Eugene moved happily through the crowds, feeding from them: from lovers, whose combined bodies made new vowels in the grass; from children unraveling from the sharp voices of their parents; from the teenage girls and boys at the riverside pubs learning the ritual of drink, mutely offering up to one another their own young bodies, as cats offer up songbirds, unaware that if you eat the song, the mornings and you will soon be silent.

Soon he shed them, continuing along the towpath, the lovely Thames slapping with the slow boats, glittering in the last sunlight. I could just keep walking along the river to the sea, he thought. He'd never be robust or brave enough for that, but what he had now was the sketchbook, virgin sheets that would lead him to another place.

Checking his watch, he saw he would be at the wharf far too early, so he sat on the bank, taking off his socks and shoes to press his feet into the cool grass. The distant murmur of the crowds recalled to him that time near the start of the war—he'd just turned thirteen—when he'd escaped from the Underground at Holborn during an air raid. He'd made his way toward his street, passing a woman lying curled in the gutter who was holding against her belly an enormous cat. "Are you all right?" he called. "Quite all right, thank you," she replied, seeming surprised he'd asked. "But if you don't mind, I'll pay you next week."

All the houses were in flames. He felt ecstatic, looking up at the stars, his world a star itself now, burning. He passed that woman again on the way back. She didn't respond when he called to her. In the slack hold of her body, the cat licked contentedly a clutch of wet kittens.

He could barely force himself back down into the Tube, its close stench of petty humanity. A fat man sitting on a stack of biscuit tins spat on the platform and regarded that pearl with sullen incuriosity. Random children played at soldiers, risking the wrath of random mothers. Suddenly one of those mothers took him by the ear and synchronized with each slap of his thigh a breathless scolding.

How debased he felt, his body numb, limp as this strange woman, his mother, pulled him to her, rubbed the dirt from his face with a licked hankie. He knew then that it was people who made other people ignoble, that this place was already shelled out, already packed with the blind and empty faces of the dead.

"You working overtime?"

Shocked out of his reverie, Eugene looked up to see Jimmy cutting across to him.

"Well, you caused quite a stir last night, my friend," Jimmy grunted out, as he lowered himself heavily onto the grass.

"Yes," Eugene replied vaguely, embarrassed by his bare feet. "I'm sorry about it. I wasn't meaning to—"

"Sure, I loved it," Jimmy cut him off.

"Give us something to chew on for a good long while."

"You know, I didn't say those things to be cruel."

"No, no, it was my fault, asking you to the pub. I should have known that Terry—"

"I couldn't help it," Eugene broke in. "All that talk—"

"What talk? You were right, we were just howling at the moon." Jimmy winked at him, but Eugene couldn't stand it, this masculine intimacy of humor and avoidance.

"When you saw me yesterday," Eugene said. "Do you know what I'd done?"

Jimmy just perceptibly winced but then seemed to resign himself, shaking his head and regarding Eugene with narrowed, anxious eyes.

"I'd got into the shower with all my clothes on."

Jimmy frowned quizzically.

"What I mean is that I forgot to take my clothes off. I stood there in the shower and didn't realize for ages."

Jimmy's face relaxed. He seemed unimpressed. "Well, I'm sure if Einstein had done the same thing, they would have said it was a sign of his genius."

There was a moment of silence. The two men looked out at the river, which was turning greasy beneath the closing vault of clouds. To the west, though, bright sun, the silhouettes of boats dissolving upon the river's blazing tongue in black communion.

"I wasn't trying to provoke," Eugene said. "I just wanted to talk, I suppose."

"Well, there are some things you can't talk about."

"Even though everyone knows them?"

"Especially when everyone knows them."

"That's just not how I am."

"Yes it is. It's how you've lived, like the rest of us."

"It is how I've lived, but it's not how I am."

"It's not how any of us are."

There was another pause.

"I begged her, you know. I begged her to marry me."

"Who? Queenie?"

"Everyone knew what we were doing. Even while William was in the house."

"But you got yourself a lovely wife in the end."

"Yes . . . for a while—but last night, I couldn't help it, in the pub. We all seemed to have failed somehow. You know, when I was young, my dad used to throw a cricket ball at me when I wasn't looking. He'd call my name when it was in the air. He wanted me to have my wits about me. I never once caught it."

"Well, that's not easy—"

"Wasn't that it was easy or not easy. What he was offering me was the chance to be a boy—his son. Like my brother, a man. And in the pub last night, when we were all looking down into our drinks, it was as if we were looking at that cricket ball on the floor. Look at Gary, his gay son, like his wife, as good as dead to him. And Terry, who's such a perfect gentleman until drink stirs up all the poison in him. William, destroyed by the war.

And Queenie married him. For what? For what? And you . . ." He stared intensely at Jimmy, who'd embraced his own legs, resting his chin upon his knees. "I read your poems with such envy. Why nothing more?"

"Ah well, it's mandatory for a Jesuit who leaves the order to write a book of poetry—especially one naïve enough to have as his reason for leaving that he'd lost his faith."

"But you—"

"No, no, you don't understand, Eugene. I'm extravagant. Forgive me, but art requires husbandry. I'm a hopeless wastrel. All those scraps, I don't know where they go, don't care; snatched up by the artist, with his busy little hands. He's a miser, a pickpocket, cheap magician; I was never cut out to be any of those things.

Which is the great irony of my life: such spiritual extravagance"—ruefully now he placed his hand upon his stomach—"such physical frugality."

"I didn't realize you'd left the Jesuits. I thought you'd—"

"Defrocked is such a silly word."

"What did you do?"

"Apart from pawning the chalice, you mean? And, of course, that incident with the girl in my chambers. Well, I discovered she hadn't been baptized, you see. There was a bath in my room. I wanted to do a thorough job—" Jimmy pulled up, glancing apologetically at Eugene.

After a moment, Eugene said, "I had a very fat friend once. I could never have a single conversation with him without putting my foot in it, mentioning fat people in some insulting way or another. That's what this thing with the schoolgirl is like. Every time anyone mentions illicit sex, people look at me as if they'd drawn attention to my deformity. And when they do that I always want to tell them the truth of what happened. That's what I wanted in the pub yesterday. To have us actually know each other before we die." Eugene paused. "Do you want to know what happened between me and that girl?"

Jimmy looked up into the dark sky, drawing the collar of his coat around his neck as a speck of rain struck his cheek. "If you want to tell me."

"Would you *care* to know?" Eugene made it an angry challenge.

Jimmy paused, frankly considering. "Yes, I would," he replied finally.

Eugene didn't say anything for a moment. This speech had run through his head thousands of times. In his flat he'd spoken it out loud, imagining his wife, or Queenie, or his mother sitting in front of him. Finally, he looked over at Jimmy, who was regarding him with a cautious but open expression, and slowly began: "Her name, as you know, was Lisa. She was one of the best—no, not the best. One of the most ardent students I'd ever had. I've never known anyone who blushed like she did. An affliction really, poor girl. But, god, it was so wonderful, when I taught, to see how captivated she was, in her face, her skin, in her blood."

"I can see you were a great teacher," Jimmy said, sincerely, but in a subdued tone, as if attempting to stem Eugene's sudden and emotional flood of words.

"I was a good teacher," Eugene said, calming himself a little. "I really was.

When I took the students to the National Gallery, crowds of people would gather round to hear my lectures. God, to think I couldn't even remember Rembrandt's name yesterday. I'd always wanted to be an artist. I'd never thought of teaching as my vocation. Never. Only after I couldn't teach did I realize how much it meant to me: to bring art to life, to open people's eyes.

"Anyway, my class was the last of the day, so Lisa and I would sometimes leave school together, take a walk in Old Deer Park. And while we were walking one day, she told me she'd never been out of London. 'Oh, we'll go to Italy,' I said grandly, 'I'll show you the Room of the Elements in Palazzo Firenze.' I didn't really mean anything, but she went quiet; suddenly took my hand. I was frozen, kept talking, but she wasn't listening, pulled me to a stop. We kissed. What an empty man. I kissed what she felt for me; I let her kiss what she believed me to be. I suppose in that way I *was* the artist. Seventeen, she was. I was forty-seven. And married to a woman I loved. I loved Catherine. As it happened Catherine was on duty at the hospital, so we went to my house. Who could forgive me? For all my dreams of being an artist to have soured to that?

"But it was hopeless. I was so confused because, in a way, she was like my child. Catherine and I had tried for all our years together to have children . . . And here was this young body right in front of me—"

"You don't have to tell me any more."

Eugene pushed forcefully on. "Here

was this young body, and a pressure in me to *realize* a nakedness in her somehow, as I imagine a father learns something essential about nakedness in the sleeping nakedness of his own child. In her body was something I'd missed or forgotten or had never understood. There we were, both naked in the bedroom I'd shared for almost sixteen years with my wife, my absence of clothes a madness, and hers—" he paused, spoke more softly. "Hers was like a mortal wound, like a dream in which a girl lifts up her dress and you can see a wound you know's going to kill her, and she laughs and runs away, and you keep trying to make her understand she's going to die." Eugene, trembling, felt himself close to tears. Jimmy, staring at the water, had turned to stone. "She was on the bed, and I remember exactly how she was sitting, like Potiphar's wife in that sad, sad painting. And I saw the back of the canvas I'd set facing the wall. It was a portrait I was working on of my wife holding a red bottle. I imagined Catherine in her starched uniform in the hospital and then—poor Lisa—I began to sob hysterically. She must have thought I was mad. I *was* mad . . . Just not mad enough.

"Anyway, so there it is, the lurid story of the schoolgirl scandal of Roehampton. That's all it came down to, a few kisses and an evening of tears. But Lisa let something slip to a friend of hers, and that friend told the nuns, and overnight I became the pervert. I lost my job, the chance ever to be a teacher again. I lost my wife."

Jimmy, hugging his own knees, remained silent for a long while. The rain intensified. At last, not turning to Eugene, but with a suddenly pensive expression, Jimmy said, "You know, I once knew a fellow called Herman. Jesuit he was, studying anthropology. Went out to Kenya to do his thesis on the Masai. Besotted with them, he was, towering warriors with their blue-black skin. Not so bad himself, very tall. But blond, Nordic, couldn't even tan. Sure, didn't he try to become just like them, living the way they lived, eating what they ate. And do you know what they ate? Blood and milk. The blood came from small nicks they made in the neck veins of their cattle. Stir it up and down the hatch. Lived on this for a number of weeks but then had to be air-lifted out in a critical condition. Do you know what he was suffering from?"

Eugene's own confession had left a buzz in his ears, Jimmy's words making sense only slowly. Finally he shook his head.

"Chronic, chronic, chronic constipation. Almost killed him. Hadn't gone for weeks. They actually had to operate to evacuate his bowels."

Again Eugene paused as Jimmy's words shunted slowly, one into another, and came to rest. "Is that a parable?"

"Why not? Nothing better than making one's filthy obsessions seem profound."

Jimmy looked towards Eugene, and both men smiled.

"Anyway," Jimmy said, "I'm off to drink some blood and milk with the rest of my tribe. What are you up to?"

"I'm going to the figure drawing. Get my hand in again."

Now both of them laughed.

"Keep your hands to yourself," Jimmy

said, slapping Eugene's shoulder as they stood.

The two men looked at one another for a moment. It seemed to Eugene that something was missing, had been forgotten. But it didn't come.

Finally, as thunder rumbled faintly in the distance, he shook his friend's hand and walked off toward the towpath. Just before he reached it, Jimmy called his name, and Eugene turned around. With a look that was at once anxious, amused, and quizzical, Jimmy pointed down at the socks and shoes Eugene had left on the grass.

FIVE

Eugene had assumed Wharf Thirteen would be part of the rebuilt dockside.

Instead it looked derelict, supported precariously above the Thames by a network of rotten beams. The storm was almost overhead; rain fell in soft sheets, and he hurried toward the entrance.

But some yards from the door, something sharp seemed to strike his temple. It made him see stars. As he recovered, he became aware again of his persistent low-level headache as one becomes aware of one's breathing after a shock. Too dizzy to move, he supported himself against the dock railing. From behind him came the quick wet clack of shoes. A young man and woman walked past, protecting their sketchpads inside their coats. The girl wore a pea coat. She was sweet-looking but for her crew cut and the crucifix that hung from a stud in her nose. The boy, tall and stooping, had a deluge of curly black hair around his pre-Raphaelite face.

The girl in the pea coat looked back at Eugene and pulled up. "You all right?" she called.

"Perfectly all right, thank you," he returned, "but if you don't mind I'll pay you—" What was he saying?

She frowned, anxious, and Eugene looked away to avoid her eyes.

"Be a soldier, darling."

It was his mum's voice. Eugene looked up. The girl was still staring at him with a worried expression.

"What?" he said.

She looked baffled. "What?" she said. "You should get out of the rain."

"I will," he said.

"Euge, you rascal," she said.

"What?" he said.

The girl, who'd started to walk over to join her friend at the wharf entrance, turned around. "What?" she called back.

"I thought you said something."

The boy hissed impatiently, "Come on, Janet. He's pissed as a newt."

They entered the wharf.

What am I doing here? What will all those artists think when they see me? A drunk, a dirty old man. He checked his watch. Eight already. The storm was getting worse. How on earth am I going to get home? Two hours, it had taken him to get here. He didn't have the money for a taxi. Why didn't I think about that? God, I just want to be in front of the TV with a cup of Ovaltine. He had to get out of the rain. The pain in his head ebbed a little, and he made his way to the wharf entrance. He noticed gouges in the rotten wood of the door frame, as if a padlocked bolt had been torn away, and wondered if the wharf was meant to be used. Just inside stood a gaunt man, well past middle age, whose features seemed to have been sculpted by years of anger. Bald on top, he'd grown the rest of his hair long and pulled it back into a pathetic ponytail. Despite the cold, he wore a sleeveless black T-shirt that exposed wiry arms bruised with faded tattoos. His skittish, furious eyes avoided Eugene's as he snatched the money from his hand.

The room smelled of wood rot and river mud. The only light came from a smoking paraffin lamp hanging above a fat armchair covered with a fraying scarlet sheet, which was the focus of a small amphitheater of folding chairs. To Eugene's relief the first few rows were filled with people who looked legitimate, many with paper affixed to portable easels, a poor man's version of Gros's studio in that painting by Masse. Everyone still wore a coat since the room was riddled with drafts, and Eugene noticed water dripping from a few places in the ceiling.

Still feeling self-conscious, Eugene seated himself in the empty outermost ring of chairs. The paraffin lamp was so dim he was in almost complete darkness, and knew he'd have to move up to the front if he wanted to draw. In the facing wall was a door from beneath which leaked a little light. The model had to be in there, wrapped up. A sympathetic shiver ran down his spine. The ponytailed man appeared at the front, his furious eyes still elusive. He clapped his hands and rubbed them together vigorously.

"Blimey, talk about suff'rin for art," he said, blowing into his fingers.

"Ain't you got no more light?" the pea coat girl called out. "I can't hardly see to draw."

"Nex' time, nex' time," the man spat back, not looking at her.

He slapped and rubbed his hands together again. "Right, we have till eleven, so we should be able get in three, four poses."

The rain surged against the roof; lightning was followed by a shattering crack of thunder that Eugene felt had burst inside his head.

The ponytailed man went to the door at the back and opened it. "You ready? Come on."

The chairs creaked as the artists made
their last-minute adjustments and rubbed
the stiffness from their cold fingers. Eugene
rested his sketchbook on his knees and
massaged both his temples, that throbbing
getting worse, sickness welling in him.

"Catch it! Got to be on your toes, boy,
always on your toes."

Eugene looked up. It was his dad.
There, right at the front, in silhouette,
stroking down the sheets of his sketchpad with the rough, drunken tenderness
with which he used to stroke the cats.
No . . . no.

The model emerged in a blue silk kimono embossed with a golden dragon,
her brown hair up in a tight bun like a
ballerina, her pert face at once haughty
and nervous. She looked so young, but
even from where he was, Eugene could see

that her feet were old, bunioned and cal-
lused. Slipping off the kimono, she quickly nuzzled her body into the armchair,
clamping her legs together and clasping
her hands over her plump, tight belly. Her
thighs were very muscular; two thick red
scars made a parenthesis around her right
knee. Barely a wisp of blond hair grew
between her legs, and the nipples of her
small breasts capped almost completely
their flesh.

The storm grew fierce. Rain beat
against the wood. Lightning illuminat-
ed a landscape of hunched backs. Leaks
sprang all across the rotten ceiling. A drip
of water landed above the model's right
eye. She cursed but stayed where she was
until the dripping became more insistent,
then she shifted just enough so the water
wasn't striking her. Her jaw trembled, and

she kept sniffing, her nipples taut with the cold. All were focused on that pale blemish over the crimson sheet, that fiercely languid almost-woman.

All but Eugene, bent double, clutching the legs of his chair, barely able to stay upon it, barely able to catch his breath. With each burst of lightning, a momentary unconsciousness struck him and seemed to purge his mind, purify it. He forgot who he was, where he was, and why—remembered, then forgot, remembered, then forgot. The sketchpad slipped from his knees, and in a moment of consciousness he reached desperately for its empty pages.

Finally, with a supreme effort of will, he managed to pull himself upright, his breath coming shallowly, a stream of rain splattering onto his leg. There was a terrible pressure in his head and a tingling throughout his limbs, which began to feel numb, as if they didn't belong to him. He heard it, then, from far away, faint at first, but growing clearer, voices, chanting, teasing. Why do they tease me?

Father's a fish man.
Father's a fish man.

Ring-a-rosie round me in the playground till I burst into fists and scattered them laughing. Dad smells of lemons, a Jack the lad, a gadabout, a dirty stopout. Mum sobs down the phone to Aunty, He stinks of other women! Lemons to cover the fish, the slippy sex. Don't say that word!

And here a bloated belly. Abracadabra, alakazam, I give you . . . a sister. My brother says it's time to celebrate. So there go Mum's cats, over the balcony, falling

three stories as graceful as leaves. It's rain-
ing cats. There goes Tim. There goes Paws.
There goes Tiny. The fabulous flying felines. What are felines? Shut up. What are
felines? Shut up. What . . . Wailing in the
boxroom; lost baby in the boxroom.

Your sister's dead
From a hydro head.

Hand pump broke. Her head burst with
water. The earth is dry. Only the tree rains
greenly.

Under the kitchen table all the chi-
na stammers like T-T-Trudy T-T-Tirrol.
Thunder, lightning, and the hum of big
black bees. The windows spray in a wave
crash. Mum shrinks smaller, Dad mum-
bles as if he's asleep. Simon mans the ack-
ack. I man the searchlights. Ack ack ack
ack! Shut up. Ack ack ack ack! Shut up.

Ack ack ack ack! For Christ's sake and for the love of God will you two shut up! The bomb didn't explode but fell

> right on his head
> killed him dead.

Never a lucky man, old Rigby. Now his wife's given birth to a sprog from every branch of the force. More semen in her than the Graf Spee, I'll tell you. The children!

> Churchill's a liar
> London's on fire.

The world's on fire. Sleek wet kittens in the woman's dead body. They steal her heat, they eat from her cheek. I'm not one of these people. The ones who will die. I am not.

I skulk about my brother's friends like

a cat lonely for a bird. Vernon shows us his dad's fingers in a jar of vinegar (all four with one Kraut bullet). How's that for sniping? Vernon says, pointing a stick at my heart. Bell Boy Binkerton has a big clapper (put it away!) and it's hairy. Simon's is hairy. They all have tarantulas in their pants. My brother's a stallion. Even Gary, who people say has already killed a man is scared of my brother. They always fight and Gary always loses. No one can beat Simon. My voice cracks. Simon takes me to the pool. He holds me to the side, subdues my spastic excitement. Wait, you little sprog, wait. Then she rises from the pool in front of us, drawing her wet hair from her face, her dark nipples visible through her cream bikini. He pinches my waist. Now, he says,

Look.

I lose my virginity with Queenie in a bombed-out house. Why won't she close her eyes when we kiss? Why does she never close her eyes?

Handsome William went to war
Handsome William is no more.

Queenie shaved her head and tried to join up. Didn't get through. Married William instead. He's her wound, a fountain with no pressure.

Damn. The war is over. London becomes the sun-squinting mass billowing from the Tube. At Chelsea Art School, I'm a fine young man. I wear a sporting jacket of herringbone tweed, smoke a pipe, and smile with sad, sympathetic irony at Van Gogh's letters to Theo, hoping she might see me.

Love. Queenie, you hurt me. The violence of jealousy as I sit before my empty canvas in Richmond Park. Sycamore leaves cluster, labial and spurious-winged, from branches flustered and rearing with leaves, fresh green, arching and trembling, the sun molten into igneous cloud, the day distilling into city lights. And in those lights somewhere, someone breaks the surface tension, a sudden yielding and slow, imaginable descent into someone else, someone touched by something less tangible, more discriminating than the wind. How could she do it? How could she not love me? How could I not be everything? I am not one of these people. I am not.

Notice, the finer the snow, the less it suffers on melting. Dogs have tongues that melt from their mouths. When Amanda's guide dog, Dillinger, died, I buried her eyes beneath a horse chestnut just blossoming in her garden. Slowly I bury my own eyes.

Why can't I be a man like my brother? Tattooed in the Navy, he smells like a man, and tells stories like a man, without fear of their reception. Such dreams I have of being in the Light Brigade upon a demon steed in a uniform the color of blood, the horses rearing and snorting. Steel them—and charge! Into the valley of death, stillness eclipsing action as one leans forward with his saber and another falls back dead with his bugle, caught forever thus. I dream of Thermopylae, of

Agincourt, of the Battle of Britain. Why couldn't I have been reborn? Take back the white feathers! But don't be so hasty. Haven't I now enough to make a bed, to lie in soft state?

Refrain: Regret.

Dad's sick. Runs away with his nurse. Nurses are sluts! Mum burns all the wedding pictures. I marry a nurse, though Catherine refuses to wear her uniform except at work. (Now Queenie, now you say you love me.) Mum won't visit. Catherine has the eyes of a cat and sucks her crucifix and eats apples too large for her tiny mouth. She collects antique bottles. And I paint her with a slow, red wound. A mortal wound. I love her, Queenie, I do. I love her because she is fragments, and then she is all the fragments together. I love her because she believes in revenge and retribution. I love her because after five years of marriage she can still look at me as if I'm a handsome stranger on the train to Brighton. I love her because after ten years I am asleep and a cool hand pulls me to my back, puts a thermometer into my mouth and a lilting voice says: Dear, oh dear, Mr. Butler, you seem feverish. Let me relieve you of your pajamas . . .

But to Lisa I quote Spengler: "In Rubens the body is not magnitude but relation. What matters is the fullness of life that streams out of it and the stride of its life along the road from youth to age where the Last Judgment that turns bodies into flames takes up the motive and intertwines it in the quivering web of active space." She understands nothing but that I am singing to her.

To the evidence against me I swore I'd done no more than replace the limp strap of her summer dress. Her father leaps across two desks to strike me, and Mother Superior removes him by his hair. I leave absolved only of my occupation and my wife, who tells me as if by way of apology that she could never have had a child.

Depressing days in the Galerie des Beaux Arts. This is my hell, shoveling swill. A year of tragedy. I fail to become an alcoholic, but my mother succeeds, and just by chance I find her dead after a week, the cats howling. While a thousand miles away Simon's shipmates, who are pretending to tread water, are shouting "Jump! Jump!" He doesn't jump but dives from ten feet into three feet of water. His friends are given a month of KP duties, and Her Majesty's Government pays for the wheelchair. Beside me at our mother's funeral sits the stallion on muddy wheels, the parody centaur, his hands black with the soil. His funeral is just a month later. In the cemetery as the priest sermonizes about self-slaughter, the sycamore seeds are a carnage of dowdy moths; they fall reeling into the grass. Queenie supports William. Jimmy seems lost. He's got another one pregnant. After being defrocked, he spent his whole life defrocking. Gary is crying like a baby. Didn't they fight their whole lives? Terry stands beside me smelling of lemons. Where is my father?

Queenie, frightened by her cruelty to William, comes to me. We spend a week in Paris. Once she had such a taut body, slim and aquatic with ribs like gills, small breasts shot with nerves, contracting smoothly under my touch, making me feel

I was sculpting her. We sit at a fountain, the shadows of pigeons moving like slow tears over an uneven face. Water spills from the broken mouths of satyrs, the punishment of excess, falling in ragged sheets over the mossy stone, falling like flames. We kiss dryly. We say it's too late.

My father was a fish man. My mother was an old woman with cats. My brother was a stallion. My wife was a nurse with no womb.

I move into a council flat, collect my bus pass and my pension. (Mr. Butler, you're a lucky man. We've managed to secure you a place in Wellington House. The woman before you had cancer of the bowels, so it needs some airing.) A living room with wallpaper of yellow roses, Messina's *Virgin Annunciate* on the wall to clean my soul, a sideboard like a great wooden jukebox upon which stand my family photographs framed in pewter, a brass Eiffel Tower, a barometer set into a rock from Land's End. A bedroom with a trolley bed, and a painting of my wife (where is she?) and the bookshelf with books to remind me of thought. A kitchen, her bottles on the window ledge, my favorite mug that has a fish tail for a handle, the wooden nutcracker in the shape of female legs, hung on a nail above the empty spice rack. A bathroom. I'm in the bathroom now, the flecks of white paint on the black toilet seat, the shaving brush in the stolen pestle. I do not reflect in the flaking mirror. And here hangs the mildewed shower curtain, rusted to the rail. I lift my arm to pull it back, but wait, no, wait. I won't do that again. Not again. This time, I remember.

* * *

It was the little model who first saw Eugene's pale foot jutting into the aisle, right at the back. The artists complained when she got up, but flinging the scarlet sheet around her shoulders, she hurried down to him. All but one sock, the old man had taken off, his clothes limp over the back of the chair beside him, his naked white body glistening wet. A thread of rosy spittle hung from his open mouth, and she noticed a blade of wet grass stuck to his bare foot. The artists gathered. A stream of rain spattered loudly right into the center of his narrow chest. Janet, the woman in the pea coat, quickly covered the old man's unmentionables with her sketchbook, preserving his modesty with the half-drawn nude of a young girl in charcoal. She could hardly bear that torrent of rain beating down upon his naked body. He couldn't feel anything, she knew, but that water striking him seemed to her a kind of pure suffering, like the suffering of an animal. This might have been because he seemed to take it so bravely, his striking Wedgwood eyes staring upwards: not with the glazed vacancy she might have expected of the dead, nor as if into a holy vision, but at something particular, unremarkable, though he was clearly pleased to have found it.

Janet would not end up pursuing art. She would lead, as she would admit herself, an ordinary life. A happy one, on the whole. One night, a few decades later, she would be in bed with her husband. They were naked and had been silent for a long while. He lay curled with his head on the soft, silky flesh of her belly, which he loved, idly running his thumb back and forth along the faint ridge of her cesarean scar.

"If you're there when I die," she said suddenly, "will you please close my eyes."

He didn't answer. Morbid, he thought.